20 Questions: Physical Science

What Do You Know About Light?

PowerKiDS press

Tilda Monroe

New York

Published in 2011 by The Rosen Publishing Group, Inc.
29 East 21st Street, New York, NY 10010

Copyright © 2011 by The Rosen Publishing Group, Inc.

All rights reserved. No part of this book may be reproduced in any form without permission in writing from the publisher, except by a reviewer.

First Edition

Editor: Amelie von Zumbusch
Book Design: Kate Laczynski
Layout Design: Ashley Burrell
Photo Researcher: Jessica Gerweck

Photo Credits: Cover, pp. 5, 7, 8, 9, 11, 13, 18, 19, 20, 21, 22 Shutterstock.com; pp. 6 (top), 12 Image Source/Getty Images; p. 6 (bottom) Cristina Merlo/Getty Images; p. 10 (top) Digital Vision/Getty Images; p. 10 (bottom) © www.iStockphoto.com/Mark Swallow; p. 14 © www.iStockphoto.com/Jozsef Szasz-Fabian; p. 15 © www.iStockphoto.com/Eileen Hart; p. 16 Kohei Hara/Getty Images; p. 17 © www.iStockphoto.com/Steven Robertson.

Library of Congress Cataloging-in-Publication Data

Monroe, Tilda.
What do you know about light? / Tilda Monroe. — 1st ed.
p. cm. — (20 questions. Physical science)
Includes index.
ISBN 978-1-4488-0672-0 (library binding) — ISBN 978-1-4488-1250-9 (pbk.) —
ISBN 978-1-4488-1251-6 (6-pack)
1. Light—Miscellanea—Juvenile literature. I. Title.
QC360.M66 2011
535—dc22

2009054450

Manufactured in the United States of America

CPSIA Compliance Information: Batch #211370PK: For Further Information contact Rosen Publishing, New York, New York at 1-800-237-9932

Contents

Good Morning, Sunshine!

Sunlight peeks through your bedroom shades in the morning. You open your eyes and look around. You see your bed, your desk, and the books on your bookshelf. If you opened your eyes in the middle of the night, these things would be only dimly **visible**. Do you know why? It is because we need light to see. We see because light **bounces** off objects and hits our eyes.

When light hits objects, it can act in a few ways. Light is absorbed, or taken in, by some matter. It is reflected, or bounced back, by other matter. Some matter refracts, or bends, light.

This girl is using the sunlight streaming through the window next to her to read a book. If you want to read a book, it is important that you have enough light.

1. Where does light come from?

All light has a **source**. For example, sunlight comes from the Sun. It travels 93 million miles (150 million km) to reach Earth from the Sun. Lightbulbs and candles produce another kind of light. These light sources are manmade. There are even some animals, such as lightning bugs, that make their own light!

Lamps, like the one this family is using, are a manmade light source. Modern lamps use electricity to produce light.

This girl is holding a candle. Candles are a very old manmade light source. People have been using them for thousands of years.

2. How does light get from its source to my eyes?

Light is a kind of **energy**. Like all energy, light is not sitting still. It is on the move! Light moves in waves, kind of like the waves you see in the ocean. These waves generally move forward in straight lines.

This glowing insect is a lightning bug. Lightning bugs are also known as fireflies. They are most often seen on summer nights.

3. How fast does light move?

When it moves through a **vacuum**, such as space, light moves faster than anything else in the **universe**. It travels around 186,000 miles per second (300,000 km/s)! However, light does not always move through a vacuum. Light moves at different **speeds** based on where it is. It moves more slowly when it goes through air, water, glass, and other matter. It is still really fast, though!

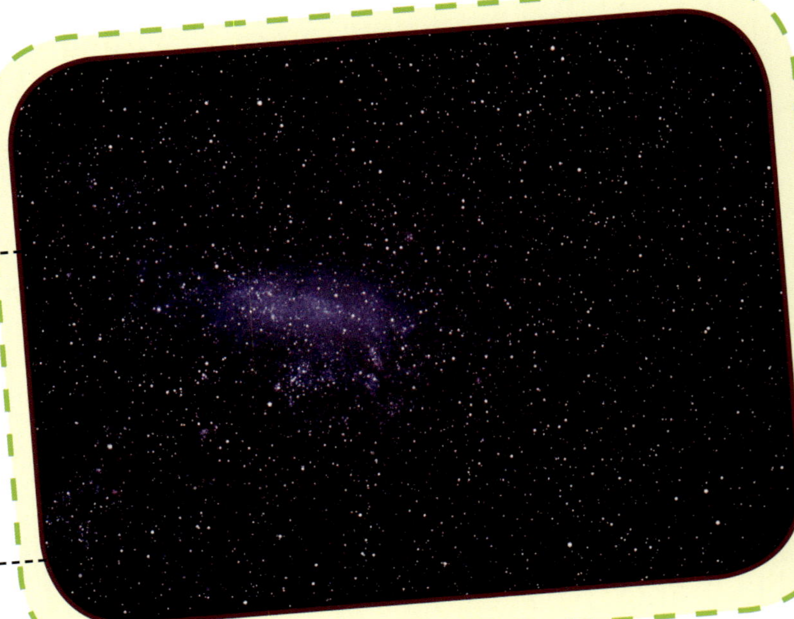

Most stars are very far from Earth. Even though light travels fast, it takes the light from these stars many years to reach Earth. This means that you are looking into the past when you look at stars!

4. Are all light waves the same?

No, they are not. The length of a wave is called its wavelength. Different kinds of light have different wavelengths. The waves that make up visible light have wavelengths between 1.3 and 2.3 trillionths of a foot (400–700 billionths of a meter).

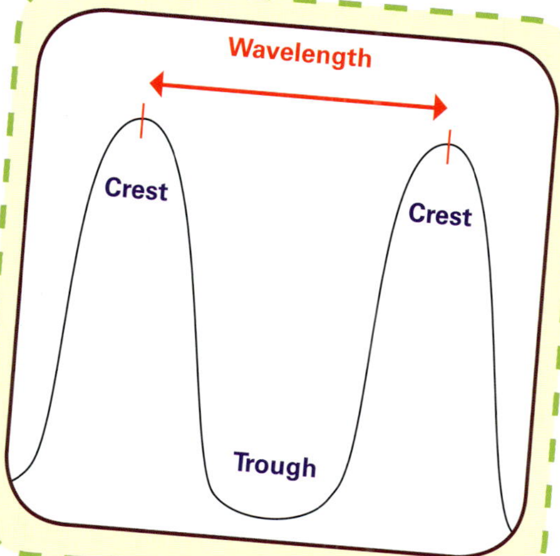

All waves have high points, called crests, and low points, called troughs. The distance between one crest and the next is a wave's wavelength.

The waves in the ocean have troughs and crests, just as waves of light do. The water moves up and down, but the wave moves straight ahead toward the beach.

5. Is the light I see the only kind of wave coming from the Sun?

Visible light, or light we can see, is only a tiny part of the energy in sunlight. There are waves with bigger wavelengths, such as radio waves. There are waves with shorter wavelengths, such as X-rays, too. All the wavelengths in sunlight make up the **electromagnetic spectrum**.

Have you ever had an X-ray? Doctors and dentists use X-rays to take pictures of the hard parts inside people's bodies, such as bones and teeth.

Along with visible light, sunlight also has other kinds of waves in it. Ultraviolet light is one of these. It can burn your skin. Sunscreen, like this girl is wearing, helps keep your skin safe from these waves.

6. Are there other differences between light waves?

Yes, light waves can have different **frequencies**. The frequency of a light wave describes how many waves pass a set point in 1 second.

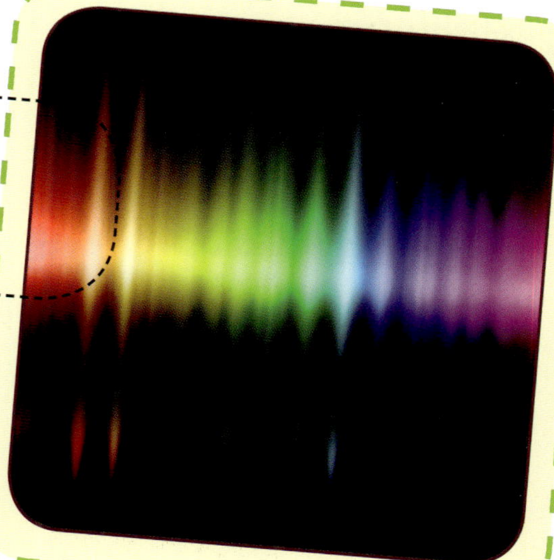

You can see the different frequencies of visible light here. In this photo, the wavelengths get shorter as you move from left to right.

7. Can I see the difference between light frequencies?

We see different frequencies of visible light as colors. Red has the longest wavelength and the least energy. Violet has the shortest wavelength and the most energy. There are seven colors in the visible spectrum.

8. If all visible light has a color, why can't I see sunlight?

Sunlight looks colorless. It is called white light. Some lightbulbs give off white light, too. White light is not really white, though. It is made up of light of every color in the visible spectrum! To see the colors in white light, we need to break up the light. This happens when light is refracted.

This boy is using a prism to break white light up into its different frequencies. You can see the colored light on his hand. A prism is a piece of specially cut glass or plastic.

9. When can I see light being refracted?

Sunlight gets refracted when it moves through a glass of water. Light of different wavelengths gets bent a different amount. This breaks the light into different colors. Sometimes, you can see the colors on your wall!

Have you ever seen a rainbow? Rainbows often happen before or after a rainstorm passes by.

10. What is a rainbow?

Rainbows happen when water droplets in the **atmosphere** refract sunlight.

11. Why does the straw in my water glass look like it is bent?

This is another example of refraction. Light slows down more when it passes through water than when it passes through air. This makes light waves change direction. To our eyes, the straw looks like it is bent.

Refraction can even make a straw in a glass of water look broken, as it does in this photo. It is making the part of the straw in the water look wider, too.

12. Do other objects refract light?

Our eyes do! They **focus** light so that our brains can make sense of what we see. When our eyes bend light too much, we need glasses. Glasses have **lenses** that bend light in certain ways to correct the picture we see. Scientists use lenses for other things, too. Lenses that are curved in the right way make objects look bigger than they are. Scientists use these lenses in tools that make small or faraway things easier to see.

As many kids do, this girl is wearing glasses. Glasses can be made to help both people who have trouble seeing faraway things and people who have trouble seeing things up close.

13. How do our eyes see?

Everything we see, we see thanks to light. We see objects like the Sun or a lightbulb because the light they give off enters our eyes. We see other objects because light from another source reflects off them and enters our eyes. Objects absorb some wavelengths of light and reflect others. This is why we can see different colors.

Everything in this picture, from grass to water to the boy, is visible because some of the light that hits it is reflected back into your eyes.

14. What kinds of matter reflect light?

All matter reflects some light. However, some matter reflects more than others. Metals and mirrors reflect lots of light. That is why they look shiny. Things with a rough **surface** scatter light, or reflect it in all directions. This makes them look dull.

Mirrors are such good reflectors of light that we can get a nearly exact picture of ourselves by looking in one.

15. Does the Moon have its own light?

No, the Moon is another example of reflected light. Light from the Sun hits the Moon and is reflected back to Earth. The Moon does not look as bright as the Sun because it makes no light of its own.

The Sun's light travels over 92 million miles (148 million km) to reach the Moon. After it is reflected, that light travels another 238,855 miles (384,400 km) to reach Earth.

16. Why does an apple look red?

As light shines on objects, the objects absorb some of the light's wavelengths. The wavelengths that are not absorbed are bounced back to your eyes. For example, when light hits an apple, light of every color except for red is absorbed. Red is reflected back to your eyes, and you see the apple as red.

Just as a red apple does, this boy's shirt looks red because all the other wavelengths except for red are absorbed by it.

17. Can light travel through objects?

Light can travel through some but not all objects. Glass, water, diamonds, and other **translucent** objects let some light pass through them. Other objects, such as your body, trees, and rocks, are **opaque**. These objects block almost all light. When an object blocks light, we can see a shadow.

Sunlight can pass easily through a translucent object, such as a glass window. However, it cannot pass through the wood parts of the window. Instead, the wood parts cast shadows, as seen in this picture.

18. Why do shadows change in size and direction?

Your shadow may be really small or taller than you are. It might lie straight in front of you or to one side. This has to do with the angle at which light is shining on you. A low angle makes for a long shadow. If the Sun is right overhead, though, you may not see any shadow!

These boys have very long shadows. Shadows are longer in the early morning and late afternoon. In the United States and Canada, shadows are longest in the winter. This is all because of the Sun's angle in the sky.

19. How do we use light?

These are solar panels. In the last few years, solar panels have become more common. They are one of the cleanest ways of making electricity.

People use light in many ways. We use **solar panels** to catch light and change it into other kinds of energy, such as heat and electricity. When the Sun is not shining, we use lightbulbs, candles, and flashlights to make light.

As all plants do, these potato plants take in sunlight and use it to produce food.

20. Why do we need light?

Without light, we could not see. Without sunlight, plants could not make food, either. If there were no plants, all the plant-eating animals would die. Then all the animals that eat those animals would die, too. We all need light!

Glossary

atmosphere (AT-muh-sfeer) The gases around an object in space. On Earth this is air.

bounces (BOWNS-ez) Moves up, down, or to the side.

electromagnetic spectrum (ih-lek-troh-mag-NEH-tik SPEK-trum) All the frequencies in which light waves, radio waves, and other similar waves can be found.

energy (EH-ner-jee) The power to work or to act.

focus (FOH-kis) To make clear.

frequencies (FREE-kwen-seez) The number of waves moving in a certain space each second.

lenses (LENZ-ez) Clear, curved objects that focus light.

opaque (oh-PAYK) Not letting light through.

solar panels (SOH-ler PA-nulz) Objects that take in and store solar energy.

source (SORS) The place from which something starts.

speeds (SPEEDZ) How quickly things move.

surface (SER-fes) The outside of anything.

translucent (trants-LOO-sent) Letting light through.

universe (YOO-nih-vers) All of space.

vacuum (VA-kyoom) A space without air or any other matter.

visible (VIH-zih-bul) Can be seen.

Index

Web Sites

Due to the changing nature of Internet links, PowerKids Press has developed an online list of Web sites related to the subject of this book. This site is updated regularly. Please use this link to access the list:
www.powerkidslinks.com/quest/light/